HEiDi HECKELBECK
and the Snoopy Spy

By Wanda Coven
Illustrated by Priscilla Burris

LITTLE SIMON
New York London Toronto Sydney New Delhi

LITTLE SIMON
An imprint of Simon & Schuster Children's Publishing Division
1230 Avenue of the Americas, New York, New York 10020
First Little Simon paperback edition June 2018
Copyright © 2018 by Simon & Schuster, Inc.
Also available in a Little Simon hardcover edition.
All rights reserved, including the right of reproduction in whole or in part in any form. LITTLE SIMON is a registered trademark of Simon & Schuster, Inc., and associated colophon is a trademark of Simon & Schuster, Inc. For information about special discounts for bulk purchases, please contact Simon & Schuster Special Sales at 1-866-506-1949 or business@simonandschuster.com. The Simon & Schuster Speakers Bureau can bring authors to your live event. For more information or to book an event contact the Simon & Schuster Speakers Bureau at 1-866-248-3049 or visit our website at www.simonspeakers.com.
Designed by Ciara Gay
Manufactured in the United States of America 0518 MTN
10 9 8 7 6 5 4 3 2 1
Library of Congress Cataloging-in-Publication Data
Names: Coven, Wanda, author. | Burris, Priscilla, illustrator.
Title: Heidi Heckelbeck and the snoopy spy / by Wanda Coven ; illustrated by Priscilla Burris.
Description: First Little Simon paperback edition. | New York : Little Simon, 2018. | Series: Heidi Heckelbeck ; 23 | Summary: Will Heidi's snoopy little brother find her Book of Spells and uncover her secret identity as a witch?
Identifiers: LCCN 2017043354 | ISBN 9781534411104 (pbk)
ISBN 9781534411111 (hc) | ISBN 9781534411128 (eBook)
Subjects: | CYAC: Brothers and sisters—Fiction. | Witches—Fiction. | Spies—Fiction. | BISAC: JUVENILE FICTION / Fantasy & Magic. | JUVENILE FICTION / Imagination & Play. | JUVENILE FICTION / Readers / Chapter Books.
Classification: LCC PZ7.C83393 Hbr 2018 | DDC [Fic]—dc23
LC record available at https://lccn.loc.gov/2017043354

CONTENTS

BUGS

Heidi and Lucy floppity-flopped onto Heidi's bed. The two best friends were playing a game they invented called Would You? Could You?

"Your turn!" Heidi said.

Lucy propped herself up on one elbow. "Okay, I've got one," she said.

"Would you? Could you? Umm, eat a chocolate-covered BUG?"

Heidi giggled and wrinkled her nose. *"Maybe,"* she said. "If the bug wasn't too crunchy. It is chocolate, after all."

Lucy gasped and squeezed her eyes shut. "GROSS!" she cried.

Both girls cracked up.

"Okay, my turn," Heidi said. "Would you? Could you? Dump a whole bottle of strawberry shampoo on Melanie Maplethorpe's head?"

Both girls squealed.

"That's funny," Lucy said, catching her breath. "But a teeny bit mean."

Heidi shoved Lucy playfully. "It's not MEAN, it's CLEAN!" she said. "Get it? *Shampoo?*"

The two girls started laughing again.

"Okay, here's a good one," Lucy said. "Would you? Could you? Ask Stanley Stonewrecker to go to a movie?"

Heidi's cheeks turned red. Then
she leaned in closer
to Lucy.

She whispered
loudly, "Yes!"

Lucy shrieked, and
both girls collapsed in laughter again.

"I knew it!" Lucy cried. "I knew it
all the time!"

Then something went *BONK* under
Heidi's bed. The girls stopped talking
and stared at each other. Heidi put a
finger to her lips. Then she hung her
head over the side of the bed and
pulled up the dust ruffle.

"Henry!" she screamed.

Henry wiggled out from under the bed. He had a huge smile on his face. He also had on a trench coat and a weird hat. Plus he was holding a magnifying glass in front of his eye.

"Super spy strikes again!" Henry cheered.

"Get him!" Heidi shouted.

Henry scrambled to his feet and raced out of the room. The girls chased him all the way downstairs.

"Mom!" Heidi yelled. "Henry was spying on us in my room!"

Heidi's mom, who had been napping on the couch, sat up and rubbed her eyes.

Heidi tapped her foot. "Please do something now!" she begged. "That Mr. Snoopy Pants is driving us crazy!"

Mom nodded sleepily. Then the girls scampered back upstairs, and Heidi slammed the door behind them.

"We should make sure your room is not bugged," Lucy said.

Heidi was worried. "Wait, you mean my room has creepy, crawly bugs?"

Lucy shook her head. "No, no, I meant a recording device," she explained. "Your little brother may be listening in—even when he's not actually in here."

Heidi looked around her room suspiciously. "You're RIGHT!"

The girls began to search. Heidi looked on her bookshelf. Then Lucy went to check under the bed. Just as Lucy started to lift up the dust ruffle,

Heidi squealed from across the room. Her heart stopped for a second as she dove to block her friend.

"Don't look under there!" Heidi cried.

"Why not?" asked Lucy.

Now Heidi's heart pounded as she tried to think of a reason to keep Lucy from looking under the bed . . . where her secret *Book of Spells* was hidden. "Because that's where I . . . uh . . . hid your Christmas present!"

Lucy sat on her heels. "You already got me a Christmas present?"

"Yes!" Heidi nodded. "Yes, I did. It's never too early to shop, that's what I always say. So you can look anywhere else in my room except under there."

Lucy dropped the dust ruffle. "Okay, but now I'm curious."

"Good," said Heidi. "Now let's use that curiosity to search for snoopy devices!"

The girls looked everywhere else, but they didn't find a single bug.

Chapter 2

SPY FOR HiRE

"Mom!" Heidi called out as she rifled through a stack of papers on the kitchen counter. "I can't find my *All About Me* folder, and I'm going to be LATE for school!"

Heidi had been working on this project for weeks. She had interviewed

Aunt Trudy about her per-
fume business and Dad
about the drink company he
worked for called
The FIZZ. Heidi

had also written stories
and drawn pictures about
herself and her friends.

She ran upstairs to check
her room again. No book. Then she
checked the kitchen and the family
room again too. Nothing. Finally she
dumped out her backpack onto the
kitchen table. It wasn't in there, either.

"It's just nowhere!" cried Heidi.

Mom lifted her head out of the recycling bin, where she'd been looking. "Think back to where you had it last."

Heidi watched a pencil roll off the table and onto the floor.

"I thought it was in my room," Heidi said. "I could have sworn that I left it on my desk so I wouldn't forget to bring it to school in the morning."

Dad stepped into the kitchen. "It's not in the mail pile either," he said.

Heidi looked at the clock. She had to go or she would miss the bus. "Merg!" she fumed. "What am I going to do?"

Henry glugged his milk and banged the empty glass on the table.

"Why not hire a SPY?" he said, wiping his mouth with the back of his hand.

Heidi scowled. "Well, if I did, I would not hire you."

She quickly shoved her books back into her backpack. Then the not-so-friendly brother and sister hurried out the door to catch the bus.

✦ ✶ ✳ ◎ ✦

On the bus, Heidi plunked down beside Bruce. Henry snuck into the seat behind them.

"What's the matter?" Bruce asked,

noticing the frown on Heidi's face. Heidi groaned and told Bruce about her missing report. No sooner had she explained what had happened than Mr. Snoopy Pants popped up in between them.

"Tell me," Henry began, "what does this missing folder look like exactly?" Then he held his magnifying glass in front of Heidi's  face. "And tell me, how many pages is it? And did you happen to mention *me* in your project?"

Heidi glared at her brother. "Why  do you care so much, Henry?"

"What?" Henry said innocently.

"You should be happy. I'm giving you free spy help."

Then he hung his elbows over the seat.

"Now . . . ," he continued, "tell me more about why some of Bruce's inventions don't always work."

Bruce's eyes grew very round. "Henry, what do *my* inventions have to do with *Heidi's* report? And, by the way, my inventions always work."

Henry held up a folder and waved it at Bruce. "That's not what it says in here." He opened the folder and read a page out loud. "Bruce is an amazing inventor, but sometimes his inventions go a little wonky, like the time he tied helium balloons to his dad's lawn chair and tried to fly it. Or the time he made an automatic dog washer and his dog, Frankie, got in the sudsing machine. . . ."

Bruce huffed. "Those inventions were still in the development stage."

Heidi grabbed the folder from her brother. "Henry, that's my report! You stole my project! You're not only a snoopster, you're a THIEF!"

Henry didn't back down. "Well, none of this would've happened if you'd hired me as a spy. Because then I would've told you exactly where your report had gone."

"It doesn't count if you are the one who stole it in the first place!" Heidi yelled.

She turned around in her seat so she didn't have to look at her brother anymore. Then she opened her folder and nudged Bruce.

"Let me read you the *rest* of what I wrote," she said.

Bruce listened with his arms folded.

"I'm so proud of my friend Bruce," Heidi began. "Because he is the most fearless scientist I've ever known.

If he doesn't get his inventions to work the first time, he keeps trying until he does. Someday he's going to invent something that will make him famous all over the world."

Bruce smiled and unfolded his arms. "Wow," he said. "I kind of like the sound of that!"

Chapter 3

SPY TRAP

"I need a SNOOP-inator," Heidi said.

Lucy laughed and tossed her the basketball. "What's a SNOOP-inator?"

The ball bounced, and Heidi grabbed it. "Someone who gets rid of snoopy little brothers." Heidi tossed the ball back to Lucy.

"Is Henry still bugging you?" Lucy asked.

Heidi nodded. "More than ever."

Lucy swished
the basketball,
before Bruce
caught it.

"Want me to
develop a spy trap
for him?" he asked.

Heidi smiled. "A what?"

Bruce held the ball under his arm.

"Well, I could try to
rig an upside-down
umbrella filled
with Ping-Pong
balls above your
bedroom door.

Then when your snoop opens the door, the umbrella would tip to one side and dump the Ping-Pong balls on top of his head."

Heidi and Lucy busted out laughing.

"And what if THAT doesn't work?" questioned Lucy.

Bruce scratched his chin. "In that case, we would have to trick him with a different way. Hmm, maybe with glue, yarn, shaving cream, and marbles."

Heidi waved off that idea. "That sounds way too messy. And with my luck, you'll trap me and not the snoop."

Lucy laughed. "Maybe you should just talk to Henry and tell him it's not nice to spy on other people."

Heidi shrugged. "Yeah, right—we're talking about the spy who listens to everything but the truth."

Then there was a really loud pop right next to Heidi's ear.

It was Melanie Maplethorpe, and she was smacking her bubble gum.

"What spy?" Melanie was completely butting in. She blew another bubble and popped it. Stanley Stonewrecker was glued to Melanie's side as usual.

"Heidi's little brother spies on Heidi all the time," Bruce told her.

Melanie laughed. "So what's the big deal? It's not like Heidi has any big, juicy secrets!"

That's when the bushes next to the basketball court began to shake. Then out popped Henry. He had been spying on them the whole time.

"No! You're wrong, Melanie!" Henry cried. "Heidi does too have secrets. I happen to know that she was going to ask Stanley . . ."

Heidi tackled her brother and cupped her hand over his mouth. Lucy faked a laugh to get everyone to look her way.

"Heidi was going to ask Stanley what his favorite color is," Lucy fibbed. "Right, Heidi?"

Heidi nodded like crazy—still holding her hand firmly over Henry's mouth.

Stanley smiled. "Fun question, Heidi!" he said. "My favorite color is red."

Melanie rolled her eyes. "Come on, Stanley," she said, hooking her arm in his. Melanie didn't like it when Stanley talked to Heidi.

As soon as they had walked away, Heidi uncovered Henry's mouth.

"Don't ever tell my secrets," she said. "Or ELSE."

Henry wiped his mouth where Heidi's hand had been.

"Well, if it wasn't for me, you'd never know Stanley's favorite color is red," Henry said. "And guess what? So is your face! And that means you LIKE Stanley."

Then Henry bolted before Heidi could catch him.

"Merg," Heidi growled. Now she had three names for her brother: Snoop. Thief. And Creep.

Chapter 4

SILENT NIGHT

Clink! Clink! Henry set the water glasses on the table. *Clank! Clank!* Heidi dropped the silverware into place. *Clunk! Clunk!* They clunked down the butter dish, the salad bowl, and the ketchup. Neither Heidi nor Henry spoke a single word.

Then the family sat down for an unusually quiet dinner. Henry didn't even laugh when Dad squeezed the ketchup and it made a bathroom noise. Mom and Dad looked at their kids suspiciously, but they didn't make much of it. They had their own things to talk about.

"The plumber fixed the leak in the basement," Mom said. "A clog in one of the drainage pipes."

Dad spooned some relish on his hot dog. "How wet is the carpet?"

Mom set down her fork. "It's not too bad," she said. "The bucket caught most of the water."

After dinner Heidi and Henry cleared the table and loaded the dishwasher—still without saying a single word to each other.

Mom brought brownies on a plate to the den for Family Reading Night. Heidi dropped onto the couch and opened her book. Henry plopped onto the beanbag chair and buried his face in his book too.

"Okay, this is getting weird," Dad said, sitting next to Heidi. "What's going on, you two? Out with it."

Both Heidi and Henry poked up from behind the book covers. Then they each began to talk at once.

"Henry is driving me crazy!"

"And Heidi calls me mean names, like Creep and Nightmare. . . ."

"Well, Henry snoops in my room!"

"Do not!"

"Do so! And he takes my stuff!"

 "Hey, I'm the one who found your lost project!"

"And he lies!"

"Nuh-uh!"

"And he tells my secrets to other people!"

Dad whistled. "Okay, time out. That's enough," he said. "I want both of you to go to your rooms and get ready for bed. We'll discuss this tomorrow."

Heidi and Henry sighed heavily and thumped upstairs. Heidi got to the bathroom first and washed her face. As she lathered the soap, she noticed

Henry in the mirror—spying on her.

"Get out!" Heidi cried, soap suds dripping from her face.

Henry screamed, "You look like a soap monster!" Then he ran away.

"Ugh!" Heidi grumbled, rinsing her face. After that, she brushed her teeth and put on her kitten pajamas. As she crawled into bed she noticed her *Book of Spells* was out and open.

"HENRY HECKELBECK!" shouted Heidi. "GET IN HERE!"

Henry scuffled across the hall in his shark slippers.

"Have you been snooping in my room?" Heidi asked.

Henry smirked and shook his head. "No way. I swear." Then he ran back to his room and closed the door. He was barely able to keep a straight face.

Heidi sighed and hopped back into bed. Henry had to be lying. *Why would a spy tell the truth to the person they're spying on?* she thought. *But what if a spy HAD to tell the truth . . . all the time? Then that no-good snoopy spy would never get away with lying or snooping again! Hmm . . . maybe a spell is the perfect anti-spy solution.*

Chapter 5

TRUTH BE TOLD

Heidi couldn't sleep that night. She tossed and turned listening for Henry's sneaky little footsteps. Finally, Heidi jumped out of bed and grabbed her *Book of Spells.* She studied the pages and found the perfect spy-busting TRUTH spell. She read it over.

LIAR! LIAR! SNOOP'S ON FIRE!

Have you ever had someone snoop through your stuff? Or perhaps you're the kind of witch who's had someone spy on you and get away with it. If you're tired of all the spying and lying, then this is the spell for YOU!

Ingredients:
1 magnifying glass
2 stretchy rubber bands
1 pocket mirror
Suspect's name written on a piece of paper in black marker

Combine the ingredients in a bowl and stir. Cover the mix with one hand and hold your Witches of Westwick medallion in the other. Chant the following spell:

SNOOPY, SNEAKY, SLIPPERY SPIES.
TELLING ALL THEIR LITTLE LIES.
BEWARE TO THOSE WHO BEND AN EAR,
SPEAK THE TRUTH FOR ALL TO HEAR!

Perfect, Heidi thought. She quickly
gathered the ingredients.

There was a magnifying glass, from inside a cereal box, which she kept in her nightstand. Next she fished out two rubber bands from her

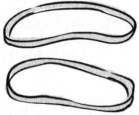

top desk drawer and grabbed a pink pocket mirror from her bathroom cabinet. Then she wrote *HENRY* on a piece of notepaper with the blackest marker she could find.

Heidi tossed the ingredients into a bowl and stirred. She placed one hand over the mix and held her medallion in the other. As she chanted the spell the bowl shuddered and the magic took hold.

Let the truth be told! she thought.

THE BLABBERMOUTH

The next morning Heidi watched her brother closely to see if her spell had worked. She didn't have to wait long. Henry began to blab the truth about everything at the breakfast table.

"You know what, Mom?" he said. "You snore."

Mom set down her coffee mug. "Don't be silly."

"No, I'm being serious!" Henry insisted. "You sounded like a huge lion snarling last night! And I know it was you because I peeked in your bedroom door."

Mom looked to Dad for support.

"Well, you know . . . snoring means you had a good night's sleep," Dad said, avoiding the question. He set a plate of scrambled eggs and toast in front of Henry.

Heidi tried hard not to laugh. She hid her face behind a cereal box.

Then Henry spoke some more truth.

"Dad, these eggs are really GROSS," he said. "They're way overcooked."

Dad's eyebrows shot up, and this time *he* looked to *Mom* for support.

"Well, you know . . . nobody said scrambled eggs were over easy," Mom said, and she winked.

Heidi could tell that her parents were beginning to get mad, so she quickly jumped into the conversation. "Hey, Henry, did you sneak into my room last night and look at my *Book of Spells*?"

Henry nodded happily. "Of course I did!" he freely admitted. "It happened last night when you were in the bathroom. You looked like a bubble monster! And it made me think— what kind of secrets would a bubble monster be hiding? So then I snuck into your room to look for a diary, but all I found was your crummy *Book of Spells*."

Heidi dropped her spoon and looked at Mom and Dad. They were not happy.

Dad pushed back his chair and wagged a finger at Henry. "This spy business will stop RIGHT NOW."

Henry looked around the table.

"Why is everyone so mad? I was only trying to save our family from the bubble monster. That's what spies do!"

Mom sighed and shook her head. "We'll talk about this whole spy thing after school. Now, have you brushed your teeth, Henry?"

"Nope!" he said proudly.

Mom pointed to the bathroom. "Brush now, young man."

Heidi watched as Henry left the table. *Wow, Mom never says "young man" unless she's REALLY mad,* she thought. *This has to be my best spell EVER!*

Chapter 7

Heidi stood outside her classroom
before school and talked to Lucy and
Bruce. Henry tugged on Heidi's jean
jacket. She whirled around.

"This is not mine," Henry said,
swinging Heidi's *Crazy Daisy* lunch
box in front of her face.

Heidi grabbed her lunch box from her brother. Then she unzipped her backpack to find Henry's *Future Spy* lunch box inside. *Did Mom prank us?*

she wondered. She handed over Henry's lunch. Then Heidi thought it would be funny to play her *own* prank on her little brother.

"So, Henry . . . ," Heidi began, "have you ever spied on Lucy or Bruce?"

Henry zipped his lunch box back into his backpack. "All the time!" he said shamelessly.

Lucy gasped. "Don't you know spying on people isn't cool?"

Henry raised his eyebrows. "Well, sure, I know! But if I had never spied on you, how would anyone know you were writing a book?"

Heidi stared at Lucy. "You wrote a book?"

Lucy blushed. "It's no big deal."

Henry waved Lucy off. "It is a big deal! The chapter I read was really GOOD."

Lucy beamed. "Why, thank you, Henry!"

Heidi coughed and almost fell over. The last thing she had wanted was for Henry to be rewarded for spying. She had to fix this. Right now.

"So, Henry . . . ," she began again, "tell us what you think of Bruce's inventions."

Then Henry happily spilled his spellbound thoughts. "Well, some of his inventions are pretty cool. But some of them are kind of weird."

Bruce's eyes grew wide. "What do you mean, WEIRD? All my inventions are totally cool."

Henry shrugged. "If you want my opinion, I'd say your spy-on-the-guy-behind-you glasses are your coolest invention. That's the best spy device I've ever seen."

Bruce's face lit up. "Well, I have to admit, I love that one too," he agreed, letting the "weird" comment go.

Heidi couldn't believe her ears. Now Bruce agreed with Henry! Her shoulders slumped, and she didn't even move when the bell rang. Principal Pennypacker walked down the hall.

"Time for class, Heidi," he said cheerfully. Then he waved to Henry.

"And kindergarten is this way," he said. "I'll walk you to class."

Partway down the hall, Principal Pennypacker looked back over his shoulder at Heidi. She quickly looked the other way.

Whoa, did Henry just say something about me? she wondered. She bit her lip. *Ugh, why does it seem like my whole spell is backfiring . . . ?*

Chapter 8

SPY GiRL

Heidi decided to keep an eye on Henry. She wanted to make sure her spell was working properly. At recess Heidi followed Henry to the sandbox. She slipped behind the bushes so Henry wouldn't see her. Then she spied on Henry between the branches.

Henry and his friend Dudley filled a
dump truck with sand and unloaded
it. Then the boys ditched the truck
and ran to the monkey bars.

Heidi crept out of the bushes and
hid behind the slide. She peeked out
and listened to the boys.

"Watch me go BACKWARD across the monkey bars," Henry said. He reached for the bar behind him and grabbed it. Then he let go of his other hand and grabbed the next bar behind him.

Heidi was so focused on her brother that she didn't see Lucy and Bruce come up behind her. Lucy tapped Heidi on the shoulder.

Heidi squealed and jumped.

"What are you doing?" Lucy asked.

Heidi looked over at her brother. Henry had seen her. He jumped down from the bars.

"She's spying on her little brother!" Bruce crossed his arms.

Heidi shushed Lucy and Bruce. What else could she do? She couldn't tell them she was a witch who had cast a spell on her snoopy brother.

Henry ran up to Heidi and her friends. "What's going on?" he asked.

Heidi tried to act normal. "Just . . . um, playing a game—that's all."

Bruce unfolded his arms. "A game called Spying on Your Little Brother."

"That's right, Heidi." Lucy nodded.

"We caught you red-handed. Why don't you tell Henry the truth?"

Heidi threw her hands in the air. "Okay, okay!" she cried. "I was spying on Henry because I don't want him to spill all my secrets."

Henry shrugged. "What secrets? It's not like I'm going to tell everyone that you're a witch or blab that you have a *Book of Spells* hidden under your bed. You can trust me on that!"

Heidi froze. Now Henry had done it. He'd spilled Heidi's biggest secret!

How could he? Heidi thought. Her face burned with anger. She looked at Lucy and Bruce to see their reactions.

Lucy rolled her eyes. "Henry, you already know it's not cool to spy on people, but it's *totally* not cool to make up stories about people!"

Bruce nodded. "Especially stories about your own sister!"

Poor Henry. He didn't get a chance to defend himself because Principal Pennypacker was on recess duty that day and overheard the whole conversation. He waved for Heidi and Henry.

"You two come with me," he said. "We need to have a little chat in my office."

The two siblings hung their heads and followed the principal across the playground.

Ugh, Heidi thought. *This spell is definitely not going as planned.*

THE MAGICAL MYSTERY

Heidi and Henry sat side by side in wooden armchairs, opposite Principal Pennypacker, who sat behind his desk.

"What's the trouble?" the principal asked. "You two aren't getting along at all. Heidi, you go first."

Heidi cleared her throat before telling her side of the story. "My brother thinks he's a spy. He snoops through my stuff, and then he lies about it, and it's driving me crazy." She turned and glared at her brother.

"Now it is your turn, Henry," Principal Pennypacker said.

"I only spy on Heidi because she always ignores me," he explained. "And it hurts my feelings.

But when I spy on her and get in trouble, at least she talks to me—even though everything she says is mean."

Henry actually cares about me? Heidi's mouth dropped open. She couldn't believe it. Something inside her softened—a little.

"Wow, Henry," Heidi said. "I never knew you felt that way. I guess I was too busy being mad at you. I had no idea you wanted my attention."

Henry looked at the floor. "Well, maybe I have been kind of a pain," he said. "I'm sorry about that."

Heidi smiled. "It's okay. Hey, if you promise to stop spying and snooping, I'll definitely pay more attention to you."

"Promise," Henry said, and Heidi knew he meant it.

Principal Pennypacker leaned back in his chair. "Well done, both of you.

From now on, though, I don't want either of you spreading rumors about each other at school."

Henry sat up in his chair. "But I was telling the truth!"

Heidi squeezed her eyes shut. *Here it comes,* she thought. *Henry's going to tell Principal Pennypacker I'm a witch.* She waited. But Henry was suddenly unable to finish his sentence.

The principal put up a hand. "Nor do I want you spreading any *truths* about each other either."

Heidi opened one eye and then the other. It felt like there was magic in the air. *Truths?* she wondered. *Is Principal Pennypacker onto me?* Heidi grabbed the arms of her chair and stood up. She looked at Henry. He looked like someone had put another spell on him.

"Thank you for letting us talk this over, Principal Pennypacker," she said, trying to block out the odd feeling in the room. "I promise Henry and I will be more respectful of each other from now on."

Principal Pennypacker winked at both of them. Then he got up and showed them to the door.

Chapter 10

HANGiNG OUT

Heidi and Henry played together all afternoon. They swept out their tree fort and brushed away the cobwebs. Then they sat down at the little table Dad had built. Heidi opened her cooler and set out two lemonade pouches and a bag of pretzels.

Henry hooked a pretzel on his finger. "You know what? I don't like hanging out with you at all."

"Hey!" said Heidi.

"Just kidding," Henry said with a wink. "This is actually really cool."

Heidi wondered if the spell had worn off or if something else had taken place back in Principal Pennypacker's office. "You're not so bad either," she told him.

They munched their pretzels and sipped their lemonade.

"Will you help me with my reading homework?" Henry asked, pulling out a book from his backpack.

"Sure," Heidi said. She scootched her chair across the floor and sat beside her brother. "You read, and I'll help you if you need it."

Henry opened his beginning reader book. "'The Spy,'" Henry began. He looked at his sister and laughed.

Heidi giggled too. "You have got to be kidding, right?"

Henry shook his head. "No," he said. "This story is actually called 'The Spy.'" He began to read:

There once was a spy.
The spy spied on
everyone.
The spy even spied on
his cat.

Nobody liked the
snoopy spy!
Soon the spy had no
friends.
The spy cried and cried.

He wanted to quit
spying.
And he did.

Now the spy is a
salesman.
What is he selling first?
His spy costume!

Heidi and Henry laughed.

"Maybe I should sell *my* spy suit too," Henry said.

Heidi crunched a pretzel. "Good idea!" she said as she gave him a high five.

Heidi liked getting along with her brother. She also liked that her secret was still safe . . . at least for now.

Check out the next book starring

HEIDI HECKELBECK

HEIDI HECKELBECK Is So Totally Grounded!

Heidi circled "Friday" on her Baby Animals calendar. *Only FIVE days until we get to see the movie,* Tristan and the Magical Toy Factory*!* Heidi Heckelbeck and her best friends, Lucy Lancaster and Bruce Bickerson, had been waiting for it to come out for months. They must have watched the trailer a hundred times.

An excerpt from *Heidi Heckelbeck Is So Totally Grounded!*

Heidi hung her calendar back on her bulletin board and went downstairs to see if anything fun was going on. As she passed the living room, she noticed the vacuum cleaner was out. *Not a good sign.* Then she stepped into the kitchen and saw a mop, a bucket, and Mom standing on a stepladder, scrubbing the inside of a cupboard.

Oh no, Heidi thought. *It must be time for the Mean Clean!* The Mean Clean was the Heckelbeck family's special cleanup day—and it always came without warning. During the last Mean Clean, Heidi had found a wet bathing

An excerpt from *Heidi Heckelbeck Is So Totally Grounded!*

suit in her dirty clothes pile. It had been sitting there for a whole week, and her clothes had smelled *super-duper* gross. She had never left her dirty clothes in a pile again.

Maybe I can sneak out of here before Mom sees me, Heidi thought. She turned around and began to tiptoe out of the kitchen. But Mom already knew she was there. It was like she had eyes in the back of her head.

"Where do you think you're going?" Mom asked.

An excerpt from *Heidi Heckelbeck Is So Totally Grounded!*